## Usborne Farmyard Tales

# PIG GETS STUCK

### Heather Amery

### Illustrated by Stephen Cartwright

Language Consultant: Betty Root
Reading and Language Information Centre
University of Reading, England

There is a little yellow duck to find on every page.

# This is Apple Tree Farm.

This is Mrs Boot, the farmer. She has two children called Poppy and Sam, and a dog called Rusty.

2

# On the farm there are six pigs.

The pigs live in a pen with a little house.
The smallest pig is called Curly.

It is time for breakfast.

Mrs Boot gives the pigs their breakfast.
But Curly is so small, he does not get any.
4

Curly is hungry.

He walks round the pen looking for something to eat. Then he finds a little gap under the wire.

# Curly is out.

He squeezes through the gap under the wire.
He is out in the farmyard.

6

He walks round the farmyard, looking at the animals. Which breakfast would he like to eat?

7

Curly wants the hens' breakfast.

He thinks the hens' breakfast looks good.
He squeezes through the gap in the fence.

Curly tries it.

He eats some of the hens' food. It is so good
he gobbles it all up. The hens are cross.

# Mrs Boot sees Curly.

Curly hears Mrs Boot shouting at him.
"What are you doing in the hen run, Curly?"

He runs to the fence.

He tries to squeeze through the gap. But he has eaten so much breakfast, he is too fat.

11

# Curly is stuck.

Curly pushes and pushes but he can't move.
He is stuck in the fence.

They all push.

Mrs Boot,  Poppy and Sam all push Curly.
He squeals and squeals. His sides hurt.

# Curly is out.

Then, with a grunt, Curly pops through the fence. "He's out, he's out," shouts Sam.
14

Mrs Boot picks up Curly. "Poor little pig," she says. And she carries him back to the pig pen.

15

# Curly is happy.

"Tomorrow you shall have lots of breakfast," she says. And Curly was never, ever hungry again.

First published in 1989. Usborne Publishing Ltd, Usborne House, 83-85 Saffron Hill, London EC1N 8RT, England. Copyright © 1989 Usborne Publishing Ltd.